THIS BOOK MORENO VALLEY PUBLIC LIBRARY
Capston
Picture W
Stone A   0000914814755

TO ORDER THESE BOOKS CONTACT:
Diana McGeorge Ph# (619) 469-9818
5920 Samuel St., La Mesa, CA 91942
Fax: (619) 465-1405
Email: gotbooks@cox.net
Voicemail: (888) 293-2609 X305

MVFOL

D0961922

A Note to Parents and Caregivers:

Read-it! Readers are for children who are just starting on the amazing road to reading. These beautiful books support both the acquisition of reading skills and the love of books.

 The PURPLE LEVEL presents basic topics and objects using high frequency words and simple language patterns.

 The RED LEVEL presents familiar topics using common words and repeating sentence patterns.

 The BLUE LEVEL presents new ideas using a larger vocabulary and varied sentence structure.

 The YELLOW LEVEL presents more challenging ideas, a broad vocabulary, and wide variety in sentence structure.

 The GREEN LEVEL presents more complex ideas, an extended vocabulary range, and expanded language structures.

 The ORANGE LEVEL presents a wide range of ideas and concepts using challenging vocabulary and complex language structures.

When sharing a book with your child, read in short stretches, pausing often to talk about the pictures. Have your child turn the pages and point to the pictures and familiar words. And be sure to reread favorite stories or parts of stories.

There is no right or wrong way to share books with children. Find time to read with your child, and pass on the legacy of literacy.

Adria F. Klein, Ph.D.
Professor Emeritus
California State University
San Bernardino, California

Editor: Jill Kalz
Designer: Amy Muehlenhardt
Page Production: Brandie Shoemaker
Art Director: Nathan Gassman
Associate Managing Editor: Christianne Jones
The illustrations in this book were created with watercolor and pencil.

Picture Window Books
5115 Excelsior Boulevard
Suite 232
Minneapolis, MN 55416
877-845-8392
www.picturewindowbooks.com

Printed in the United States of America.

Library of Congress Cataloging-in-Publication Data
Klein, Adria F. (Adria Fay), 1947–
Max learns sign language / by Adria F. Klein ; illustrated by Mernie Gallagher-Cole.
p. cm. — (Read-it! readers: the life of Max)
Summary: Max takes a class in sign language so that he can talk with his friend,
Susan, who cannot hear.
ISBN-13: 978-1-4048-3148-3 (library binding)
ISBN-10: 1-4048-3148-7 (library binding)
ISBN-13: 978-1-4048-3545-0 (paperback)
ISBN-10: 1-4048-3545-8 (paperback)
[1. American Sign Language—Fiction. 2. Deaf—Fiction. 3. People with
disabilities—Fiction. 4. Hispanic Americans—Fiction.] I. Gallagher-Cole, Mernie,
ill. II. Title.
PZ7.K678324May 2006
[E]—dc22   2006027565

Editor's note: To learn more about sign language, check out these books:
Heller, Lora. *Sign Language for Kids.* New York: Sterling, 2004.
Holub, Joan. *My First Book of Sign Language.* New York: Scholastic, 2004.
Price Hossell, Karen. *Sign Language.* Chicago: Heinemann Library, 2003.

1.4

Max
Learns
Sign Language

by Adria F. Klein
illustrated by Mernie Gallagher-Cole

Special thanks to our advisers for their expertise:

Adria F. Klein, Ph.D.
Professor Emeritus, California State University
San Bernardino, California

Susan Kesselring, M.A.
Literacy Educator
Rosemount–Apple Valley–Eagan (Minnesota) School District

PICTURE WINDOW BOOKS
Minneapolis, Minnesota

Max and Susan are good friends.

Susan cannot hear. She is deaf.
Like many deaf people, she makes
special signs with her hands to talk.

Max wants to learn how to talk with his hands.

7

Max takes a sign language class after school. The teacher signs, "Hello."

Max signs, "Hello," too.

The teacher shows Max the sign for *friend*. He teaches Max a lot of signs.

The teacher gives Max a book about sign language.

Max signs, "Thank you."

Max takes the book home. He practices the signs for *park* and *bike*. He practices other signs, too.

14

park

bike

The next morning, Max sees Susan
in the hall. They both make the sign
for *hello*.

17

Max makes the sign for *friend*.

Susan makes the sign for *friend*, too.

Max asks Susan if she wants to ride her bike to the park.

Susan signs, "Yes!"

Susan teaches Max new signs every day. Max and Susan are good friends.

23

More *Read-it!* Readers

Bright pictures and fun stories help you practice your reading skills. Look for more books at your level.

Max and the Adoption Day Party
Max Celebrates Chinese New Year
Max Goes to a Cookout
Max Stays Overnight
Max's Fun Day

Max Goes on the Bus
Max Goes Shopping
Max Goes to School
Max Goes to the Barber
Max Goes to the Dentist
Max Goes to the Library

Looking for a specific title or level? A complete list of *Read-it!* Readers is available on our Web site:
www.picturewindowbooks.com